Bonnie on the Beach

by **Susan McCloskey**

illustrated by **Steven Roberts**

D.C. Heath and Company
Lexington, Massachusetts   Toronto, Ontario

One day Bonnie went to the beach.
The sun was warm. The sea was blue.
It was a beautiful day!

Bonnie went for a swim. She dived
under the water.

When she came up she saw...
A BEACH MONSTER!
But was it really a monster?

No! It was only Alice playing in the water.
There is no such thing as a monster.

Bonnie got sleepy. She lay down
on the sand and closed her eyes.

When she opened them she saw...
A BEACH MONSTER!
But was it really a monster?

No! It was only Gus flying his kite.
There is no such thing as a monster.

Bonnie went for a walk. She walked
backwards so she could see her footprints.

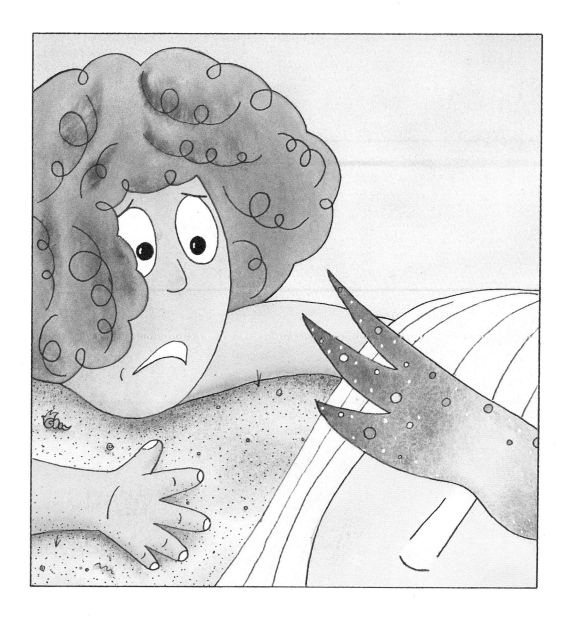

She tripped over...
A BEACH MONSTER!
But was it really a monster?

No! It was only Meg buried in the sand.
There is no such thing as a monster.

Bonnie looked for shells in the sand.
She found some pretty pink ones.

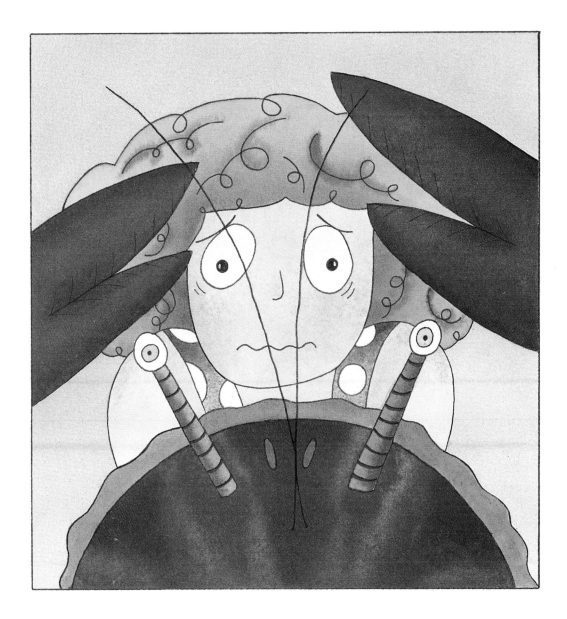

When she looked up she saw...
A BEACH MONSTER!
But was it really a monster?

No! It was only Gus chasing her
with a crab.
There is no such thing as a monster.

OR IS THERE ?